Albert Gallatin Riddle

Mark Loan

A Tale of the Western Reserve Pioneers

Albert Gallatin Riddle

Mark Loan
A Tale of the Western Reserve Pioneers

ISBN/EAN: 9783337120276

Printed in Europe, USA, Canada, Australia, Japan

Cover: Foto ©Andreas Hilbeck / pixelio.de

More available books at **www.hansebooks.com**

MARK LOAN

A Tale of the Western Reserve Pioneers

———

By the Author of " The Hunter of the Shagreen."

———

CLEVELAND, O.
WILLIAM W. WILLIAMS
1884

TO FLORENCE

IN MEMORY OF HER LAST DEAR HOME-STAYING.

May 1, 1884.

CONTENTS.

I. THE PIONEERS - - - - - 9

II. THE GOLDEN RULE - - - - - 11

III. MARK - - - - - - 12

IV. THE SHADOW - - - - - 21

V. THE POET - - - - - - 25

VI. GOD'S WAY - - - - - - 33

VII. ANN - - - - - - - 38

VIII. THE FLOOD - - - - - - 43

IX. MARK LOAN'S SPRING - - - - 48

X. HIS MISSION - - - - - - 62

PUNDERSON'S POND - - - - 65

MARK LOAN

A Tale of the Western Reserve Pioneers.

I.

THE PIONEERS.

Far from the older eastern world remote,
  Walled round by western forest shade profound,
Warring with nature wild, the fathers smote
  The huge trees, whose fall, with wide resound,
Shook the virgin earth.   On that distant ground
  They made their homes.   Theirs was a moveless age,
Time stood still as slowly they wore away
  The forest.   Ceaseless, stout the war they wage,
Nor genius nor high thought called into play ;
  Nor books nor journals—culture small had they,
But clear'd land, tamed steers, hunted, wove, spun ;
  Wore their dull lives with toil, waiting the day
Of better things, higher life—so they run
Their weary rounds, till all their days were done.

I know that was a rude, hard primal life,
  Such as all men live " in the beginning,"

When hand and thought are constant in the strife
  For existence, which they are ever wringing
From surroundings harsh ; to which the soul is bent
  And body given.   Yet memory more kind
Hath, in the passing years, with sweet intent,
  Lost all the loveless things ; and now I find,
On all within her arms, the wondrous play—
  The light of that old and seeming better day,
Shining with serene and steady ray ;
  Nor shadow, nor mem'ry of darksome night,
  Nor sorrow, grief, nor pain, nor any blight ;
  But all lies sweet and sacred in that light.

II.

THE GOLDEN RULE.

Those were the days of endless toil;
Each waking hour had its moil.
Whose mem'ry reaches that time olden,
Recalls this as the sub-rule golden.

" The greatest thing of all is work,
    The greatest man the greatest worker ;-
The meanest of all things is shirk,
    The meanest man the greatest shirker."

Hard was the rule, the working hard,
    For outer man, for inner worse;
The form was bent, the soul was marred,
    The mind grew sordid 'neath its curse ;
Yet no man, woman, child might draw
Themselves from reach of this stern law.

III.

MARK.

In that old world was never known
A boy so idle as Mark Loan.
It was not that he wanted grace ;
   Harmless he was as child might be ;
Seemed ever he was out of place,
   Unless beneath a wild-wood tree,
Living a part in his own dream,
   Rapt in another world away ;
In our life did it ever seem
   He had no part for work or play.

The Loans were thought a common band ;
The men were all of griping hand ;
Close, thrifty, given all to delve,
To grub with hoe, or axes helve;
Of old and young were ten or twelve.

The girls hard working, decent, plain,
  Good folk to grapple with the wood ;
Dull witted, sun-browned.   In the main
  With their neighbors not ill they stood ;
  Tho' little known for ill or good.

Poor Mark was with the younger fry ;
With them—not of them; how or why
He was found in their common brood
All wondered.   His seemed other blood,
Of other mold, another race ;
Large, dreamy eyes, blond, girlish face ;
Tall, slender, having much of grace ;
Shy and gentle from his birth,
Pensive, sad, never showing mirth ;
From the first counted of no worth.
Useless his hands for daily toil,
  'Twas not so much that he would shirk,
As that he was not born for moil.
  To him the common, coarse, hard work
Was not assigned.   This understood,
  Quite young an outcast Mark became;
Neither stripes nor yet want of food

Gained him to work.   Prison nor pain
Won aught from him save patient tears;
Nor murmured nor did he complain,
When bidden from their board remain,
And hungred he would steal away
To his own world, the lonely wood,
Ling'ring there the live-long day.
From nature's hand he sought his food;
He was her own well favored child;
From his stepmother, him she took
To her breast, nursed him in her wild
Ways of life.   Taught him where to look
For meat and shelter ; him she made
One of her own loved, cherished throng
Of children, dwelling in the shade
Of her great wood.   Him, led along
Her secret ways, by stream and glade,
Nothing fearing, none were afraid
Of him—a harmless, graceful thing,
Whose form filled them with brutish awe;
Yet naught of terror did he bring,
But by sole force of *the great law*,
His presence ruled.——

———The deer would feed
  At his side, turning great soft eyes
On him.   The timid doe would lead
  Her fawn across the leafy mead,
And meet him there without surprise.
  The partridge drummed beneath his eye,
The turkey-hen still kept her nest
  If there, by chance, he passed it by ;
Or where he went, or sat at rest,
  Unfrightened stole the wild things shy.
Of rav'ning things he had no fear,
  Nor bears avoided more than deer.

He knew the ways of all wild things,
  Their homes and haunts ; of all the birds,
Where each one built, the note it sings
  Yet ne'er betrayed by sign or words,
Them to the hunters of the wood,
  Who often in its solitude
Met him wand'ring beneath its shade,
  Or by the feet of old tree laid.
He loved the trees—each greenwood tree,
  As if 'twas planted by his hand ;

He loved the plants, and watched to see
    Them prink in spring through all the land.

He loved to wander by the stream
    And list its murmur; on its banks
Lie cloud-gazing, as in a dream,
    Where the great trees stood thick in ranks.
'Twas grief to have a tree cut down ;
    He could not bear to see one fall ;
'Twas woe the forest to discrown ;
    He loved the trees, the wild things all;
The humblest plant that budded there
Was object of his love and care.

No creeping thing that there had birth ;
    No insect floating in the air
On filmy wing ; what ere the earth
    And sun gave life, his kindred were.
All living things to him were joy ;
Nor any life would he destroy
Of any thing beneath the sky ;
Nor would he see a creature die ;

Nor of any slain would he partake.
With tender care guarded his tread,
Lest 'neath his foot 'twould be the fate
Of some tiny thing, its life to shed.

So loving, tender, large his heart,
  Throbbed warmest for his human kind ;
Though in our world he had no part,
  And in our love did never find
Return. From the first misunderstood,
Banned from birth by kindred blood;
Who gave him being in him found
Something scarce of human kind;
Dark words and hints from them went round,
Poisoning much the vulgar mind.

On their hearth sat a withered crone—
A half-witch wife—old granny Loan ;
Malignant foe of Mark was she,
  And would have had him left to die ;
And such, quite sure, his fate would be,
  But that a sister, furtive, shy,
  Did his childish wants supply,

And often on her tender head
The curse of his was freely shed.

"Thou dost not work and shalt not eat,"
The mandate stern, oft did repeat
The father of the churlish band
To the poor boy, as oft his hand,
    And oft his voice drove him away
From food, as from the shelt'ring roof,
When all turned from him aloof,
Save the loving sister—tender Ruth;
By stealth scant scraps to him supplied,
When stricken was the girl and died.
Henceforth for him were rags and scorn,
Nor kindly none, since that sad morn.
The old crone to them all declared
That poor Ruth's fate was due reward
For her transgression. God had bared
His arm to punish. Full regard
By all the rest was duly paid
To the mandate of the cruel head.
That day the father's will was law
    To all the household, old and young.

None dared obedience withdraw,
  None questioned mandate of his tongue.

When there lay his dear Ruth in death,
Mark saw that came no more her breath;
That moveless was her tender head,
And came to him that she was dead ;
  Well nigh his life was rent away;
No word he spoke, no tear he shed,
  But in a deadly stupor lay,
Not knowing what was said or done;
  While the blank hours passed away
They placed him in a loft alone.

The neighbors gathered from the wood ;
  A prayer was said, a hymn was sung,
As by Ruth's open grave they stood ;
  And ere the evening shade had come
Her form was hidden in the clay,
  When to their cabin homes they past,
  None saw Mark, none for him asked.
A hunter, at the close of day,
  Came near the freshly-made small mound,

And there, half naked, near it lay
　The poor boy Mark, upon the ground;
He lifted him and bore away
　To his hut.　Had met him in the wild,
　Knew something of the lonely child.
　There many days did Mark remain,
　And something of his strength regain.

IV.

THE SHADOW.

Little of Mark to us was known ;
　　A wand'ring, weak and harmless lad,
Crazed and driven forth to roam
　　By perverse spirit, lone and sad.
None knew the course with him at home ;
Small dealing was there with the Loan,
Who dwelt where few 〔had cause to roam.
'Twas said that Mark was crazed and strange,
　　That nothing for him could be done,
'Twas given him the wood to range,
　　A curse upon the Loans said some ;
A working out of some weird fate
　　That filtered in their sordid blood.
That once a youth of higher state
　　Had loved a daughter of the brood.
There was mishap in olden time,
　　And a great wrong was somewhere laid ;

This Mark was latest in that line.
  Granny Loan something of this said ;
And there was that in the child's form
And eye, something by him worn—
  Some confirmation of the tale
Men saw.   Many strange things were told
  Of the boy.   Some said there was a veil
On his face at birth, and legend old
  Of its portent.———

  ———To watch a stream
  Often had he been known for hours,
And so the clouds—as in a dream ;
  List'ning the voices of the wind ;
  Joy in the swish of leaves could find ;
Passion strange had he for flowers ;
  Would lie all day for song birds' note,
Watch a woodpecker drill a hole ;
  Unheard voices seemed to float
On the air, for him.   Fragrance stole
  On the breeze to him alone ;
  His ways were strangest ever known.

For him all boys had sorest scorn ;
　He would not work, a coward was,
'Twere best that such had not been born—
　The stern award of all their laws.
If he ventured—as he some time
　Into their presence did—coarse jibe—
Something in boy's rude, rough line—
　Assailed him.   Some of the brutal tribe
Called him names—"coward," "girl-boy," " shirk ;"
　Set smaller to jeer him.   ''Crazy,''
" Lived on bark and roots ;" "would not work ;
　Would starve first—he was so lazy."
When grew the storm hard he betook
　To flight ; ran to the nearest wood.
Useless pursuit, so swift of foot ;
　Their cry reached not his solitude.

To him the girls were ever kind ;
　His wistful look and gentle voice
In their tender hearts could alway find
　Response.   In their presence no choice
Was left the brutal, coarse and rude ;
　To them he made his mute appeal,

Though ne'er on them did he intrude,
    But rather from them would he steal.

His favorites were children small ;
    His presence soothed their grief, alarm,
As gently on their forms did fall
    His hands—soft were they and a charm.
The mother with her clam'rous fry
    Was glad to have him on her floor ;
The youngsters, with a joyous cry,
    Haled him to the cabin door.
Though some said ill luck followed him,
    As his own shadow, vague and dark ;
They quoted tale of poor Ruth's sin,
    Nor deemed it wise to favor Mark.
Nor favor at any hand he sought,
    And seldom he accepted food ;
If ere he did he always brought
    Return—something from the wood—
    Herbs, whose charm he understood;
Prickly ash, Virginia snakeroot,
Something as a return he took.

V.

THE POET.

As fruitage of his father's rule,
The poor boy never went to school,
Though often to the house he hied
And lingered on the outer side;
Was drawn there, almost every day;
Yet as for him no one would pay,
He could but stand with wist mute look
At what, for him, was sealed up book.

Sweet girl Ann the school once taught;
   Saw him there, noted him well;
The boy within the house she brought,
   And this the story which they tell.
   She placed a book within his hand
   And bade him on the floor to stand—
Strange thing, as all the children thought;
   Yet stranger that which followed there;

Mark read the lesson—read it well—
  Yet how he learned to read, or where,
No one knew how it befell.
  'Twas in his heart to learn to write,
And the next day did with him bring
  Some graceful feathers, gray and white,
Shed from the shy wild goose's wing.

Quick through the settlements it ran :
  Mark Loan was going to the school;
And word was sent to schoolma'm Ann
  That this was plain against all·rule.
Some said 'twas shame to teach a fool;
  Some said 'twas shame to drive away
A harmless, helpless, simple lad.
  Much talk it made, but every day
Ann found him pensive, silent, sad,
  Waiting to follow through the wood
  Her steps to the log hovel rude,
  Where she taught girls and smaller boys.
The larger in the summer time
  Were kept at work, and no annoys
Met Mark in that girl gentle throng,

And quick the summer passed along.
For her kindness, at later day
The thoughtful girl Mark lived to pay.

In that rude time to read and write
The end was of all learning quite;
That and learn to add, subtract,
    Divide by rule and multiply.
To Mark these were an occult act,
    Which he beheld with wond'ring eye.
Meaning none for him they had ;
    And when, by oft and serious test,
Ann found the strangely fashioned lad
    Took no thought—not the slightest rest
Found they in his soft mind and strange ;
They were beyond its utmost range ;
    And when she marked his growing years—
His tall form, eager, wistful eye—
    She could not refrain her woman's tears.
The youth, unknowing, silent shy,
Wondered to see his idol cry,
And never comprehended why,

But wept. For her his tears were shed,
Wond'ring what to them had led.

He worked with such an eager will
That in short time he had some skill
In use of his good gray-goose pen,
Which gave him greatest joy, and then
It was known why the penman's art
Had been so eager sought by Mark.
God placed it in his heart to sing ;
    There lit the true poetic fire ;
In every vein he felt its sting,
    And in his soul its flame would pyre.
Long time he'd felt it like a pain—
    Felt long ere yet he heard the voice—
Yet, when he caught the sweet refrain,
    Its meaning knew, did great rejoice.
It was the first, the only joy,
On the path of the lonely boy.

When sure this thing was all his own,
In him the thought was quickly grown—
He needed aid of ready pen
    To inscribe his lines, perfect his song.

No thought of fame, no thought of men—
But carry his high themes along.
When first they grew beneath his eye,
True fashion taking from his hand,
Wings they seemed, on which to fly
In raptures sweet, in soarings grand.

He wrote his lines upon the trees;
He wrote them on the autumn leaves;
On the inside of elm tree bark
He wrote them with a stylus sharp,
Formed from hard and pointed bit
Of wood; with what would mark he writ.
As poets have of every land,
He wrote them in the fading sand;
Wrote on forms of yielding clay,
As poets wrote in oldest day.
What ere from hand would impress take
His hand inscription sheet would make.
Paper there could few command,
Save scraps and bits ; none in the land.

Mark translated the songs of birds,
Put what to him they sang in words.

The wind's low moan was in his strain;
The tinkling voices of the rain
Fell soft and sweet in his refrain.
The woodland stream that rippled on
Lent its murmur to his song;
The pleasant wash of summer wave,
   Nature's voices, each sweet sound,
Its accent pure to him gave,
   And in his simple strains was found.

No model had he, none had seen
   No poesy, no bit of song;
To dwellers of that forest green
   Did no true poet's work belong.
There only were Watt's dreary hymns,
   From which he turned, as all bards do.
His flowing lines were not born twins,
   Not thus did brooks and rivers flow.
He seldom tagged them out with rhyme,
For none he saw in space and time;
None in David, in Isaiah none,
Nor smoothly did their numbers run.
No feet were there in waft of leaves,

Wind blown ; none in the voice of breeze ;
Unequal measure had the days,
   None had the glory of the stars ;
The sun in couplets sent no rays ;
   The great wind anthems knew no bars ;
The thunders rolled, the lightnings flashed,
Forests were rent, the great waves dashed;
Onward, varied, grand and wild,
   Or murm'rous, sweet and soft and low ;
Fitful or plaintive; so this child
   Heard nature rythmic ; his song's flow
Was cadenced, and continuous ran
   Its wild strains, or they fitful broke
Musically and without span,
   In pearls, as the oriole's note.

In Mark men noted a great change
From grief to joy, and said 'twas strange ;
At his lines were sore amazed ;
Declared the youth was surely crazed.
To average men the bard is crazy;
Even good men look on him as hazy.
Poesy was our latest gift ;

The land a dearth, the time was long
Ere came a poet in the drift
Of our dull years of sordid thrift ;
   And faint and slender the first song,
   Which welleth now free, full and strong.

VI.

GOD'S WAY.

God sends a prophet; none know it,
He goeth; few are half aware;
  A singer,—men don't know a poet,
And for his office have no care.
    Few can for him see any use;
    Of time his calling is abuse.
God sends them in his time and way—
  Time and way both—to men strange seem;
No warning given of their day;
  Few men hail them when they are seen.
They come and sow their precious seed;
  They come and sing or say their word;
Save the wind, no one hath heed;
  Have no thought, have nothing heard.

Man's fortune is in his own hand;
  For good or ill God shows no care,

Save sowing his oft barren land,
  And leaving all with man to fare.
Men must this lesson surely learn,
  Grow quick to see, acute to hear ;
To such the high One seems to turn,
  His purpose loving, his teaching clear.
Of all a poet's, one simple song
  Toucheth men's hearts, assuageth strife ;
Of all seed sown, the earth along,
  One germinates a tree of life.

The Messiahs are never known ;
  To be rejected, their sure fate ;
None are received—not any one,
  Came he early or comes he late.
Alway are they out of time,
  Alway are they out of place ;
And yet their mission is divine,—
  For those who scoff them, winning grace.
The untrue prophets are believed,
And the Messiahs false received.

Mark's simple strains most men derided,
  No meaning in them ere they saw ;

Nothing caring, he abided,
  Steadily working out the law;
Gaining strength and, with years older,
More sure his grasp, his utt'rance bolder.
Something vaguely some were guesssing—
Something had he, something possessing ;
Yet what it was, could no one tell ;
A spirit that should with them dwell,
To inner self appealing solely ;
That self larger, higher, holy,
Which enibraced all other selves
Reaching beyond the self that delves.

In his verse winnowed by the wind,
Things strange and high did some men find ;
Setting stars in their long night ;
Showing new thought in their new light ;
To things obscure dimly showing,
Idea of all things rythmic flowing ;
Not disjointed, cursed and broken,
But of purpose giving token.
Some glimpses of diviner beauty
  Making harmonious the whole ;

Showing love the soul of duty,
  And beauty essence of the soul.
Something of this to some he taught,
  Some little light to darkened day;
Some kindling of diviner thought,
  Sending here and there a ray;
  Showing there was a better way
Than the slav'ry of ceaseless toil.
The sordid curse of grovelling moil
  Might be lifted, lightened up;
Work might be means and not man's bale;
  Need not be poison in the cup,
  From which the sons of men must sup
And die, and life of no avail.

Something of this to younger few
Mark's riper songs gave slender clew.
The music of their murmurous flow,
  Their rhythm caught some attuned ears,
Gentle, tender, plaintive low—
  Maidens they beguiled to tears.
Sweet, delicious, 'twas to cry,
And so they wept, not knowing why.

So, as his years ran deep'ning on,
He sang a deeper, stronger song.
He thought not of their meaning, sense;
His lay was its own recompense.
So idly he seemed to sing,
Like thrush in thicket with closed wing;
Sufficient for the day to him.

VII.

ANN.

Ann was that young hunter's wife ;
  In time to her was given a babe ;
And in the woods she lived the life
  That others lived within its shade.

Matrons and maids were brave and free ;
  They walked the forest paths alone,
Nor feared beneath the greenwood tree
  By day, that danger ere could come.

Taking her babe one summer day,
  Along the trail went matron Ann,
To her mother's house, it led the way ;
  Through tangled wood and glade it ran.

When in the middle of the wood,
  And near the path, upon the ground,
The funniest thing of forest brood,
  Sleeping in the sun she found.

Black and fuzzy, shapeless, small,
A funny little rolled up ball;
Nothing like it ere had she seen,
So cunning, harmless did it seem,
That, thoughtless, she her child laid down,
And took the wild thing from the ground.
It oped its small, black, bead-like eye,
And piped a feeble baby cry,
Answered by fearful growl and crash
Of limbs, as with leap and dash
A fearful, monstrous, shaggy thing
Broke on Ann, who back did spring ;
Dropping the cub in awful fright,
As the rageful creature met her sight.
By her own babe she dropped it there,
And o'er it stood the mother bear ;
On her hinder legs, strong, upright,
Angry, growling, fierce for fight,
In defense of her recovered young ;
    Leaving Ann's untouched, as unseen.
Ann in horror stood, unstrung,
    Saw it there, as in fearful dream.

Ere yet to her came back her thought ;
And save the fierce bear saw she naught ;
There flashed upon her daz-ed sight
A vision, as of angel bright.
Mark Loan her trembling form leaped past,
And snatched her babe in sure grasp
From the ground, the raging bear beside,
Saying to her some word of chide,
And bore it where Ann, drooping, stood.
    The bear not long cared there to 'bide,
With her cub scrambled through the wood.
To Ann, each now free-drawn breath
Was recov'ry of her babe from death.

Mark had many a cherished nook—
    Resorts, for him—well loved places,
In forest wild, by pond or brook,
    Where the shy, elusive graces
Hovered unseen in their wild sport,
And held with him their greenwood court.

Parts of old deserted, grass-grown roads,
    Where bright-winged things flashed in the beam,

Cathedral woods, silent abodes
  Of shadow, where no ray was seen ;
As was his mood, so each he sought,
For musing light or deeper thought.

To-day, while lying prone along
  The mossy bank of rippling brook,
List'ning to its liquid song,
  And watching how the sun rays strook
The limped current, changed its sheen,
  Lighting white pebble, moss-grown stone,
The water-cressets crisp and green ;
  Hearing the wood-flies' drowsy drone ;
When tearing through the frightened wood,
  Breaking from the fierce brute throat,
With its dread threat of death and blood,
  Came the she bear's rav'ning note.

The dreamer's long trained ears alert,
  Knew what the cry did well presage ;
Skilled in the ways of beasts, expert,
  He sprang to rescue from its rage.

He took Ann to her mother's door
And lingered till her stay was o'er,
And guarded her to her own home.
Twice glad the task to young Mark Loan
That this thing came for him to do;
Ann's husband was the hunter true,
Who came in time his life to save
And bear him from his sister's grave.

VIII.

THE FLOOD.

That summer Mark had reached nineteen,
  And later came the awful flood ;
Like it no thing had ere been seen
  By white men in the western wood.
The Loans one morn were on an island,
And fast diminished their small dry land;
From the sky a drowning deluge pour'd ;
'Round them a swelling torrent roared ;
On either side a raging river
  Them from help and hope did sever.
No aid unless the awful Giver
  Should stay the flood; that, or never
Would they escape.   A cowering band
  On their low roofs they helpless stood ;
Not stout of heart, nor deft of hand,
  Powerless to battle with the flood ;
Men and women, children, babies,

Helpless as children where no aid is.
And higher as the water rose,
 They crowd the loft, then climb the roof
Of their wide cabin. Seemed near the close,
 Still hope and help were far aloof;
Naught but cries, incoherent prayer,
Ghastly faces and wild despair ;
When stepping from a slight, frail bark,
Among them bravely stood young Mark.

 He set at once to form an ark,
That burdened by the helpless brood
Should bear it safely o'er the flood.
His form, his acts, revived their hopes ;
 Some aided in what he would do ;
The stout roof-poles he lashed with ropes,
 Boards and *shakes* were tied thereto;
With ready wit and rude, deft craft—
 Taught him by his hard, wild life—
There floated soon a buoyant raft,
 With strength to ride the angry strife
Of the on-sweeping, boiling tide.
 On it he placed the children small,

In the centre placed, side by side ;
　　Women next, men last of all,
Ranged 'round the rest, and each did call
　　By name and counted, so that none
Might be left. With care the crone
　　Was by him placed, when every one
Was embarked, on the sweeping tide,
Mark saw the float might safely ride
The watery space to hard, high land,
　　Not far below if drifting right ;
He cast it off with his own hand,
　　And guided in his shallop light.

He bent his force, lent all his skill,
　　Giving to it his utmost might,
To overcome the current's will.
　　Small help he had. Some of the band
Gave slight aid, but his the skill
　　Brought the shapeless craft to land,
On the slope of a sweeping hill.
　　With fearful tugs, many a strain,
　　And often had all seemed in vain,
Mark his float stranded, made it sure,

And landed of the tribe of Loan,
From largest to smallest, all secure,
   The youngest babe, and bell-dame crone—
Fifteen in all, I've heard them say ;
A pallid throng, at close of day.

The rain ceased, the clouds broke away,
The sun sent his last yellow ray
O'er the swollen on-going flood,
Which now ran smooth where the huts stood ;
Of cabin chimney, stick nor stone
Was left to meet the ray that shone.
The settlers of the higher land
   Heard of the peril of the Loan,
And hurried on from every hand
Too late to aid save at the strand.
Loudly they cheered heroic Mark,
And helped his crew from their rude ark.

Idle as useless to try and tell
The words—the acts—which there befell.
When they landed, that strange voyage o'er,
On that hillside, the strangest shore ;

Rescued by Mark, the outlawed child,
From peril so great, so strange and wild;
Young night was in the leafy wood.
Neighbors gave them rest and food,
Led them to their log cabins near,
And shared with them their homes and cheer.

IX.

MARK LOAN'S SPRING.

Sweetly and fresh the morning broke,
  On field grown large, on lessened wood;
Along each marge the song birds woke,
  And all together poured a flood
Of melody, a fount each throat ;
  Each strove to make his own song good.
On the side of that wooded slope,
  Unseemly in the morning ray,
A stranded drift Mark's rude craft lay ;
From it the flood had ebbed away,
Leaving it there to mark the place,
Unsightly thing, that once bore grace.

A dimple sweet in the hill's side,
  A simple cup for crystal spring,
Spilling there its murmurous tide ;
  Whimp'ring down a silv'ry thing ;

In cascades leaping on its way,
  Beneath the umbrage of the trees,
In its rill the sunbeams play
  With shadows of the forest leaves.
Mark had known it when a child ;
It was remote, secure and wild.
Often thither his tender feet
  From his sordid kindred stole away ;
It was his earliest retreat,
  And held its place to later day.
Few knew of the loved, lonely thing ;
By them it was called " Mark Loan's spring."

From his landing to this loved dell,
  In the young night, weary, o'ercome,
Mark stole away, and drooping fell
  By the spring's margin dear.   No one
Saw or missed him.   There alone,
In the deepning shade, he dropped and slept,
While at his head the waters wept ;
Their teary sobs were in his brain,
Solving, soothing his voiceless pain ;
Nature, his mother, in her wild

To her bosom clasped her child,
If he woke, hushed to sleep again.

He slept the lonely hours through,
What visions came none ever knew,
Nor of him none had thought or care;
His great true mother with him there,
Cared and lulled, her voice he hears,
Her low sobs, and he knew her tears.

Sleeping through the sweet, holy night,
Sleeping through the clean morning's light;
Wakes not to hear the hermit thrush,
Which to hear, other singers hush;
Hears not the sweet, low wash of leaves;
In fingers of the fanning breeze
   They wave and clap their green, cool hands;
And the great shadows of the trees
   Come out and move in solemn bands
On the hill's side; still doth he sleep,
And still the sobbing waters weep.

The shy, wild things about him creep,
   Wondering that he riseth not;

Birds, with their heads turned sidewise, peep
　At the known form in the loved grot,
Curious, as still grows the day,
He sleeps, while sunbeams o'er him play.

That morn tripped forth Ann's young sister,
　Well liked the day, and like it laughed;
The level sunbeams met and kiss'd her,
　As the sweet morning's breath she quaffed.

Round, bare, brown arms, and bare, brown feet,
　Rosy-lipped and fresh and ruddy,
Blue-eyed, lithe, tall, seventeen and sweet ;
　She found the bare earth sodden, muddy.

From a near cabin others came,
　Girls—some younger, and some small boys,
By concert, walking down a lane,
　The lads shouting, making much noise,
As boys will.   Going through the wood
To see the course of the great flood.

Of the Loan adventure they had heard,
And of Mark the girls had a word—

Many—to say.   No one knew where
  He was.   Last seen on that strange shore,
Landing his helpless kindred there;
  When their perilous voyage was o'er
He disappeared.   This was the last,
Nell said, and that some way he passed
From them.   He was a pleasant theme
  To these maidens—he was to Nell,
And as they pass'd the wild wood green
  She talked of him, had much to tell;
His task performed, he stole away
  To some wild, dearly-loved retreat;
  She would not wonder should they meet
Him somewhere in this very wood.
Then at length the young girls stood,
The stranded raft of Mark beside;
They wondered that the fearful tide
Should reach so high, now sunk so low,
And shrunken to its usual flow.

Nell's eyes searched eagerly around;
If aught they sought, they nothing found,
If hidden wish her heart indulged,

To her mates naught her lips divulged.
Of Mark Loan's spring the maiden knew,
  And to it once the girl had been ;
Now quick and keen her glances threw
  Over the hill side, for its stream.
Along the slope she led the way,
Nor far did their young feet stray
  When its shining thread was seen.

Upward they followed eager Nell,
  The tiny, silvery thing along ;
The small glen deepened toward the well,
  Whence came its mimic liquid song.
There, under the maiden's searching eye,
  The extended form.of him she sought
Still on the moss-grown bank did lie.
  Her friend's hand in her's she caught,
And pointed to the drooping form
Of Mark, there in the green wood lorn ;
The fountain still its waters wept,
And on its margin still he slept.

The maidens stole with silent feet,
As not to break his dreamless sleep,

With hushed breath and not a word,
   Until they wond'ring near him stood ;
Naught save the lisping spring they heard,
   And zephyr breathing in the wood.
In maiden cheeks the blood grew warm,
As 'neath their eyes the sleeping form,
Nude to the waist, flashed on their view,
Fair and lovely as ever grew
The fairest maiden. They silent gazed,
And as they looked were sore amazed.
The head laid back, 'neath it an arm,
   O'er which lay the long, light-brown curls ;
One cheek, on which the sun smiled warm,
   Round, soft ; the shoulders as a girl's ;
The lips bare, severed. There the charm
   Of innocence, as pure and sweet
   As if they'd found a girl asleep.
So wondrous fair, so dazzling white,
Giving to day a purer light ;
And over him the sun and shade
In mystic dance weird gambols played.

Nell from her slender waist untied

Her spotless tire, stole to his side ;
'Twas not that she his form would hide
From their girl eyes, but from the day—
From the sun's kindling, deep'ning ray.
As she bent down she gave a start,
As something said—" this is not Mark !
The casket this ; Mark is away
To other realm of brighter day."

She marked his breast, she noted well
'Twas moveless—neither rose nor fell ;
Marked the mouth, that through its cleft
No breath passed—it was bereft.
Starting, she threw up high her arm,
Raised her voice in wild alarm :
"He is dead !   He is dead !" she cried,
And sank her there down by his side.

" He is dead !" was caught by the breeze,
That told it to the list'ning trees ;
The trees told it to all the birds ;
The birds bore wide the startling words
To all the wood things, to each stream,
In all the realm of wildwood green,

Till in each sweet, wild place 'twas said,
In accents sad, "Mark Loan is dead."

Wide-eyed the pallid children stand,
'Round Nell, a mute and frightened band,
Sense of uncomprehended harm ;
Of death, its awful mystic charm.
A moment—she turning to them said :
"Go—tell ev'rybody Mark is dead."
Not long ling'ring did they stay,
But hastened through the wood away ;
All save Sue, Nell's chosen friend,
Who staid with her the dead to tend.

Nell, with her 'kerchief, washed the face,
Then did her pure white tire place
   O'er him.   Washed his hands, wiped all trace
From the sleeper's bare, brown feet,
Making them pure, clean and sweet.
Not far the lower earth they trod,
And of it bore no stain to God.

They set green boughs to hide the sun,
Then, when their thought had all been done,

They sat them down, as women would,
And added tears to th' weeping flood ;
That flowing ever would ever weep,
While the young sleeper e'er would sleep.

The young day had not grown to noon,
When hast'ning through the woody bloom
Came the settlers—they all came,
    From near and far, the old and young—
Women, children—did none remain.
    A sad-faced, wond'ring, silent throng,
They came, and 'round the dead amazed
They stood, and on the wonder gazed ;
Him, the weakling, the youth half crazed ;
Marked the broad, high-swelling dome
Of his young head ; there was a throne,
A temple, abode of vision, thought ;
Great labors there might sure be wrought.
This now they saw—not seen before ;
So much of the true prince it bore,
As one sprung from a royal race ;
Plainly marked on his head, his face.
An angel's they seemed now, when death

From those pure lips had stolen breath
Had placed there with his marble seal
   The impress of his mission high,
Token that did to all reveal
   That something from the upper sky
Was given him on earth to bear,
He'd borne it, and was silent there.
Knew a prophet had been sent them,
Priest of nature had been lent them,
And was gone.   Rev'rent they bent them
And sadly.   He came—was gone ;
None knew him—not any one ;
Had walked the virgin earth alone.
Whate'er his work, it was all done,
His message spoken, yet had none
Heard it, save as sighing breeze,
Fanning the unknowing leaves,
Or dropping rain when nature grieves.
Or had he found the earth so drear
   He could walk it but little way?
Alien, cold, he would not stay here,
   So turned him to celestial day.

Then the mould which he left behind,
    Wrought of the divinest earth,
On which these rude men now could find
    Signs of his celestial birth,
They tenderly prepared for clay.
    Old men wept the common loss,
There they laid him at close of day ;
    Maidens strewing flowers and moss,
Tear-dewed in his damp, cool bed.
In silence there they laid his head
In that dear place he loved so well;
Where the first ray of morning fell,
Day longest lingered in that dell;
The sweet, rich southward-going slope,
Where the young tide of spring first broke.

There him they left with fading day ;
Silent the folk then stole away.
The thoughtful, in the dark'ning green,
Pond'ring what this thing might mean ;
But most of all, why had he come ?
What had he said, what had he done ?
More perplexing—why had he gone ?

And so in maze they pondered on ;
And this in their minds o'er and o'er,
To them a problem, was full sore;
They turned vexingly on each side,
Why now—now immature he died?
Why smitten in these early hours,
Ere his growing buds were flowers?
No word spoken, nor any deed,
Save this last, that could ripen seed.
Some slender lines, washed by the rain,
　Nor color had, as by the breath
Of spring in winter—but these remain,
　And the spoiling hand of death.

Faintly as in our latest day,
At the summit of earth's highest way,
Where, with rapid, steady, sure beat
Of mighty wings, his stainless feet
Stood to rule, the sceptre bearing ;
Him all former deeds preparing
For greatest trust.   Lo, it is written,
In that high hour was he smitten !

A nation's hope, a people's trust,
A name, a mem'ry, ashes, dust!

Christ's life was greater than his teaching,
    His death was more than his whole life,
Example than life, death, preaching;
    Of all things the sum was that rife.

It is God's work, and his the plan;
    He useth men and lays them down;
He explains naught to any man—
    His angels bear a cross or crown.

They left Mark in his best-loved wood,
    Where weirdly the soft summer night
Wove mystic shadows, making good
    Her reign.   Later the moon's thin light,
From leaf to leaf there dripping down,
    Rested on the new placed stone,
In form fantastic, a pale crown
    O'er the young head laid there down.
And ever the sad waters weep,
Drowsily, through the sleeper's sleep.

X.

HIS MISSION.

Of things men set their hands unto—
The idlest work they ever do
Is to set over fallen head
A monument, carved for the dead.

A life is its own monument,
　　Sole that with man can ever dwell;
It showeth forth its own intent;
　　Its purpose own alone can tell.

Mark's was a glimmer, a fine ray,
　　Of the better, the diviner sight;
Gilding that hard, that sordid day,
　　Soft'ning, sweet'ning, by its pure light
Bringing out the hidden meaning
Of many things hard, dark seeming,
Showing rhythm in discords sore,
And beauty where none was before.

The gift of genius is to see
    Things to which other men are blind ;
His labor, make translation free
    Of vision to our common mind.
Knows the relations of all things,
    Their true inter-dependence seeing;
All to the rule of order brings
    By the law of its own being.
The poet sees the lines of beauty,
    The true harmony of all things;
Harmony, rhythm, everywhere,
These he sings, as is his duty—
    Rhythm, beauty his songs declare.

Something of this Mark Loan saw,
    Something he showed to those near him.
Beginning were a few to draw
    Within the charm, glad to hear him.

From his sweeter, fresher life,
    Grace on their hard lives was shed ;
Sweetness to the bitter strife
    Of their days for bitter bread.

For his life their lives were better,
  Hope in his young songs was found ;
Larger, lighter, grew the fetter
  With which their sordid lives were bound.

He was very much to lovely Nell,
  Much more may be than she knew ;
More, surely, than ere did she tell,
  As into womanhood she grew ;
Womanhood of finer type,
  Formed by soft air and sweeter dew,
And day of broader, purer light,
  To which Mark's songs and life were clue.

He, one of the unknown singers,
  His song unknown, unheard his name,
One of many unnamed bringers
  Of good that brings to them no fame.
So he lived, so passed away,
Bearing some light of better day.

PUNDERSON'S POND.*

In the pulsing heart of the deep old wood,
  Held in the arms embracing of the hills,
Wild crystal mirror of the solitude,
  Daughter of hidden springs and filtered rills,
  Of rains and dews, which the clean earth distils,
Thou didst from morn to dewy falling night
  Give back the trees, whence the wild thrush trills
Fell on thy breast, where played the sheeny light,
And forms of stately swans, who there stayed their flight.

In thy reeds the wild mallard reared her brood ;
  In thy tide the loon bathed his mottled breast ;
The antlered buck and his doe, from the wood
  Came to drink of thee; the wild goose to rest
  Sunk on thy bosom.   When adown the west
Fell the late sun, the red-winged blackbird came
  With his rich notes.   Night brought many a guest.
The fire-flies around thee soft lit their flame,
Through the night the whip-por-will did to thee complain.

---

* Read at the reunion of the pioneers of Newbury, on the eastern
shore of the lake, August 22, 1882,

Thou hast seen on thy shore the Indian camp,
    His birch canoe thy crystal tide upbore,
At night streamed over thee his torches' lamp;
    The dusky maiden when the day was o'er
    Met her brown lover on thy dark'ning shore;
On thy bosom they saw the stars' soft sheen.
    All these have passed away, and never more
Shall the Indian boat on thy tide be seen,
Yet its memory shall ever haunt thee, like a dream.

From thy southern rim thou dost still outpour
    Thy spilling waters, in a lovely stream,
Though grandly on thy hilly banks no more
    Stand the great crowning ranks of trees in green ;
    Dower'd with beauty as a fadeless queen,
Whose loveliness survives the loss of crown,
    The light still plays on thee in changing sheen
Now as ever.   Not older hast thou grown
But in a fresh glory shinest ever thine own.

There came a youth* from out the older East,
    King born, large-brained, broad, strong—the self same
        hour

---

*Lemuel Punderson in 1808.

He saw he loved thee,   Not thy beauty, least
   That attracted.   He saw not thy dower
   Of rare loveliness; it was thy power
To serve his man's needs, drive his wheels, his mills—
   Thy out-running stream was thy sole flower;
He marked where that ran wild among the hills,
He measured, estimated, all thy feeding rills,

And grasped them—all thy wooded hills and thee—
   Made dominion of all the land around;
The axmen came: the forest, tree by tree,
   Fell beneath their blows with great resound,
   The shy spirits of the ancient profound
Startling from all their hiding places,
   Breaking the wooded wall that once thee bound,
Thy flood turned into new earthy races,
Raw, till Nature came to clothe them with her graces.

Came a hunter,* man of gigantic mould,
   With great swart brow, who slew on thy shore
Elk, bears, and deer.   Others, young and old,
   Came with their rifles, pushed their rude boats o'er
   Thy bright wave; shot thy wild fowl till no more

---

*Welcome Bullock.

The swan sought thee, and the wild goose grew shy—
And fishermen, not fishermen before,
Learned in thy depths the easy rod to ply,
Drawing from thee of thy innumerable fry.

Many households of the new race of men
Came, and built their cabins through all the woods,
War waging on the long ancient reign
Of Nature; broke up all her solitudes;
Dissolved forever the wild charm she broods.

They beheld thee—they and their children came
To look on thy lone beauty; chief of goods
The forest held; as the wild world grew tame
Thy changeless loveliness for them did still remain.

Along the banks of thy outflowing stream
Walked lovely women—they stood on thy sands
And smiled to look out over thy bright sheen,
Held thy lilies in their once lily hands,
Browned with the toils of their new life, with bands
Of eager children standing there with them,
Whose shouts thou heardst—heard through all the lands;
You took them to your arms, became their gem,
Wooing the wanderers to thy embrace again.

Thou sawest again the youthful lover
    On thy bright margin woo the maiden shy ;
Standing coy beneath the forest cover,
    Turning from him to thee her conscious eye ;
    Held in reluctance sweet that would not fly,
And shame-faced listens as she would not hear
    Words, sweetest that on woman's heart can lie,
Tremulous lest there should be ling'ring near
Companions, who might catch accents to her so dear.

As the memory of a child's bright dream
    Do I recall my vision first of thee ;
Through opening trees did thy waters gleam,
    Sparkling blue under June's sun.   Around me
    Were mothers, children ; before us I see
Lithe men and boys pushing a new-made boat,
    A canoe, fashioned from a tulip tree,
Wrought by my father's hand, which deftly smote
Our first shapely craft, that did on thy bosom float.

Strong doth the scene in living colors lay
    In mem'ry, a picture perfect.   Thy blue,
A flash of dimples, green leaves, the bright day,

The eager-watching group—in shading true,
  In changeless, fadeless form as ever grew
On canvas, 'neath painter's eye and hand ;
  Light and shadow perfect—still do I view ;
And more than picture—I see the bright band
Launch—spring into the boat, and push her from the land.

Men and boys in the boat, rowing from shore,
  Is the last, living ever in my mind ;
Going from me, I see them.   Never more
  Turns that prow back ; and never can I find
  Anything in mem'ry with it combined,
Before or after.   It stands there alone ;
  No joinder has to things of earthy kind.
Many such things of life have I known,
Which my child mind siezed—·and forever holds its own.

From that day the lake a part of my life
  Became—grew on me, as with years I grew.
She was my pastime ; her dear shores were rife
  With things which stir boyish hearts ; a view
  Of her sent a thrill my young bosom through.
I loved her long, as lovers sometimes do,

Not knowing why.   Often 'mid falling dew
  I stole to her ; marked as did upper blue
Change, she changed ; gave back to it, star for star, in answer true.

  At that hour a deep joy it was to stand
    Alone, under the trees, on her weird shore
  As the still night its charm wrought in the land,
    And spread its veil of mist her bosom o'er ;
    And feel a spirit rise not there before,
  Solemn and sweet, that wrapt my being round,
    Making me one with Nature; which did pour
  Into my heart her essence.   Silence, sound,
Life and death, were science of the Great Profound.

  O, oft and oft have I stolen away
    Through the wood, gliding 'mid the darksome trees ;
  To stand on her still shore, at close of day ;
    To feel the weird spirit, that round her weaves
    At eve its spell.   That thing which to her cleaves,
  In which voices of water-haunting things
    Are harmonies—drop as from Summer eves
  Dews drop, and notes that the whip-por-will sings
Are the plainings, which the sad soul of night there brings.

Once again the links of that broken band,
    That so brightly in the long buried years
Stood in strength and beauty on thy white sand,
    Silently gather on thy shore, in tears ;
    Marking how in each other's forms appears
The change wrought by the graving hand of time.
    We mark no change in thee, time thee endears.
Eternal loveliness thy gift divine ;
Thy first smile 'neath the Creator's hand still is thine.

A poem thou, written by God's finger,
    Spread in the hills to win the souls of men ;
We turn—cling to thee, and still we linger,
    And going—turn back to thee once again ;
Thy loveliness as fresh as that time when
    Our eyes thee first beheld, loth to sever
Them from thy dimpling blue, Eternal gem,
    Whose light and hue shall fade from thee never,
That thing of beauty which is a joy forever.

www.ingramcontent.com/pod-product-compliance
Lightning Source LLC
Chambersburg PA
CBHW031242260626
47169CB00007B/2413